# The Lucky Duck Song

To welcome Tom Deering
into the world
*November 1992*

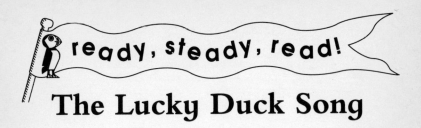

# The Lucky Duck Song

Martin Waddell
Illustrated by Judy Brown

Puffin Books

PUFFIN BOOKS

Published by the Penguin Group
Penguin Books Ltd, 27 Wrights Lane, London W8 5TZ, England
Penguin Books USA Inc., 375 Hudson Street, New York, NY 10014, USA
Penguin Books Australia Ltd, Ringwood, Victoria, Australia
Penguin Books Canada Ltd, 10 Alcorn Avenue, Toronto, Ontario, Canada M4V 3B2
Penguin Books (NZ) Ltd, 182–190 Wairau Road, Auckland 10, New Zealand

Penguin Books Ltd, Registered Offices:  Harmondsworth, Middlesex, England

Published in Puffin Books 1993
10 9 8 7 6 5 4

Text copyright © Martin Waddell, 1993
Illustrations copyright © Judy Brown, 1993
All rights reserved.

The moral right of the author/illustrator has been asserted

Filmset in Monotype Bembo Schoolbook

Reproduction by Anglia Graphics Ltd, Bedford

Printed in England by Clays Ltd, St Ives plc

Lucky Duck was a duck who
thought BIG. She wasn't a feed-
me-please duck like her friends.

"I'm going to be a Song-Writing
Pop-Quacking Star!" she told the
Big Ducks on the pond. "I'll be
the very first duck-from-our-pond
to appear on TV in her own show
and I'll win lots of Gold Discs with
my songs!"

"Don't be a daft duck!" the Big
Ducks told her.

They ruffled their feathers and swam round the pond quacking loudly. They were telling the world they knew a duck who was crazy.

Lucky Duck got very cross.

She waddled out of the park and
down the High Street, where she

bought a tiny guitar from a shop.
Then she waddled back to the
park, with her guitar slung on her
back.

"I've got a guitar!" she told the
Big Ducks. "I've got a guitar and
I'm going to play it and quack!"

That set them scolding again, but
Lucky Duck didn't care.

"Ducks from our pond don't play guitars!" they all told her. "And pop songs aren't duck-like! You'll make us look silly!"

Lucky Duck didn't listen.

She signed up for lessons-by-post
to teach her to strum her guitar.
She practised all day, far away
from the pond, where the Big
Ducks couldn't hear her.

Practice made perfect.

She wrote her very own tune by the light of the moon, and she added her very own words.

She called it the "Lucky Duck Song".

It went like this:

THE
LUCKY DUCK SONG

QUACK QUACK QUACK
QUACK
QUACK QUACK QUACK
QUACK QUACK QUACK
QUACK
QUACK QUACK QUACK!

There were several more verses, all much the same.

One bright sunny day Lucky
Duck went back down to the
pond. She stood on a bench by the
side of the water. She quacked her
song, and played her guitar.

19

The Big Ducks didn't listen. They swam round the pond with their bills in the air pretending that she wasn't there. "That duck's a disgrace to our pond!" they quacked.

Lucky Duck didn't care!

The Big Ducks didn't like her song, but the Ducklings loved it. They came out of the water and gathered around the bench. They

ruffled their feathers and flapped
their wings and tapped their tails
on the ground to the sound of the
Lucky Duck Song!

The Ducklings were dancing
about on their webbed feet. They
were having a ball, quacking
along to the Lucky Duck Song.

# The Big Ducks were worried!

They ganged up and chased all
the Ducklings away, scolding and
waddling the way Big Ducks do.

"What's the idea, Lucky Duck?"
the Big Ducks asked. "Whoever
heard of a duck-from-our-pond
quacking a stupid duck song?"

Of course they were WRONG,
but they didn't know it! They had
pondweed in their ears!

"Some ducks are born to quack on the pond and some ducks are born to go far," Lucky Duck quacked.

"Some ducks can get out of our park!" quacked the angry Big Ducks. They chased Lucky Duck away from the pond, biting her bottom with their big bills.

Lucky Duck hid in the bushes with her guitar, all tattered and torn. She was too sad to quack any more.

She waited till night, when the park-keeper was gone and the Big Ducks were out of the way. Then she slung her guitar on her back, climbed over the fence and waddled away from the park.

Poor Lucky Duck! The streets of a
city by night are no place for a
duck out of luck. There were cars
and big lorries, and people out
walking and talking.

They laughed when they saw a
small duck with a guitar trying to
climb on to a bus, and they
shouted at her.

Lucky Duck ended up by the bank of the river. She spent the night under a bridge. There she met Alma Cat and the Kittens, singing their song to the moon.

The song didn't sound like a hit,
and Alma Cat knew it. Alma was
a cat who was cool.

Lucky Duck started to quack!

Alma Cat purred with pleasure.
She flipped off her bin lid,
swinging her tail!

"Sign up with my band, Duck, and I'll make you a star!" she miaowed.

And Lucky Duck did!

The next night they all played a
big show down at the dump.

"You have to start somewhere!"
Alma Cat said. Lucky Duck knew
she was right.

Alma sang, the Kittens played.
Then Lucky Duck stepped on the
stage.

Lucky Duck was nervous and
scared, but Alma Cat pushed her
into the spotlight.

"You can do it, Duck!" Alma Cat
purred. "You're not just any old
duck-from-the-pond, and you'd
better believe it!"

Lucky Duck shut her eyes, and she
P-L-A-Y-E-D, quacking the
Lucky Duck Song.

No one had ever heard a duck-
from-the-pond quacking a song
like the Lucky Duck Song on the
roof of a car in a dump.

The crowd were amazed. They
stopped dancing and talking. They
all gathered round to hear the
new sound.

"QUACK QUACK QUACK
QUACK
QUACK QUACK QUACK
QUACK QUACK QUACK
QUACK
QUACK QUACK QUACK!"

The crowd began cheering and
dancing about. They all joined in
the Lucky Duck Song, yelling and
shouting for more.

That was just the beginning.

Lucky Duck went on TV. She had her own show, backed by the Kittens, and Alma on drums.

Lucky Duck made it B-I-G,
topping the charts everywhere she
played! Lucky Duck was a Star!

She travelled the world with Alma and the Kittens, singing the Lucky Duck Song. She made lots of Gold Discs and lived on hotel swimming-pools.

And then, with the world at her quack, Lucky Duck went back to the park. She flew in her own helicopter, *Duck One*. She brought lots of bread for the Ducklings (AND the Big Ducks as well), and spread it about on the pond.

The Big Ducks were sorry they'd chased Lucky Duck, and they said so. They told Lucky Duck they'd been wrong.

"Never mind," Lucky Duck quacked. "Whoever heard of a duck-from-our-pond quacking songs to the world?"

And they all joined in quacking the Lucky Duck Song!

Most of the Big Ducks got it
wrong. They quacked out of tune.
The Ducklings were much better
at quacking their quacks to the
beat of Lucky's guitar and Alma's
drums.

The Ducklings all knew she'd go
far (for a duck-from-the-pond).
and Lucky Duck did . . .

. . . quacking the Lucky Duck
Song.

ready, steady, read!

*Other books in this series*